THE NIGHT PARADE

by Lily Roscoe

illustrated by David Walker

All rights reserved. Published by Orchard Books, an imprint of Scholastic Inc., *Publishers since 1920.*

ORCHARD BOOKS and design are registered trademarks of Watts Publishing Group, Ltd., used under license.

SCHOLASTIC and associated logos are trademarks and/or registered trademarks of Scholastic Inc.

Library of Congress Cataloging-in-Publication Data

Roscoe, Lily, author. • The Night Parade / by Lily Roscoe ; illustrated by David Walker. -- First edition.

pages cm   • Summary: In the Night Parade children play and sing while their parents sleep.

ISBN 978-0-545-39623-3 (alk. paper) -- ISBN 0-545-39623-9 (alk. paper) 1. Night--Juvenile fiction.

2. Parades--Juvenile fiction. 3. Imagination--Juvenile fiction. [1. Stories in rhyme. 2. Bedtime--Fiction.

3. Night--Fiction. 4. Parades--Fiction. 5. Imagination--Fiction.] I. Walker, David, 1965- illustrator. II. Title.

PZ8.3.R669Ni 2014 • 813.6--dc23 • 2014008922

10 9 8 7 6 5 4 3 2 1   14 15 16 17 18

Printed in Malaysia   108 • First edition, September 2014

The art was created using watercolor and ink.

The text was set in Chaloops Decalf. The display type was set in Pupcat.

Book design by Chelsea C. Donaldson

For Teddy, Walter, and Nate,
the kings of my Night Parade
—L.R.

Especially for the ever-growing
Lillis family
—D.W.

Have you ever wondered what happens at night
while mothers and fathers lie sleeping?

Children wake up.
They climb out of their beds,
some crawling, some
running, some leaping.

As the moon shines down they escape into town.

To the Night Parade they go sneaking . . .

Have you ever been to the Night Parade,
where children dance under the stars?

The streets are all empty, no grown-ups in sight
as they skip around signposts and cars.

Their voices rise high

as they sing to the sky

sweet songs about faraway places.

They make cakes for the moon
with an old wooden spoon
and get frosting all over their faces.

Have you ever been to the Night Parade,
where children play games in the dark?

They build castles of sand.
They paint pictures by hand.
They turn somersault
flips through the park.

Ringing bells, stamping feet,
banging drums to the beat,

flying banners
of silver and blue.

They wear costumes and hats,
bark like dogs, purr like cats,
holding hands as they march two by two.

Have you ever been to the Night Parade
where children read mountains of books?

They circle around, falling soft to the ground,
nestling closely to have a good look.

They tell magical tales
about mermaids and whales
and creatures who live in the deep.

But with each happy ending
there is no more pretending.
The children are falling asleep.

No more laughs, no more screams.

They are ready for dreams.

The Night Parade comes to an end.

As dark turns to dawn,

the boys and girls yawn,

and say good-bye to their friends.

Without a sound
they are homeward bound,
waving up to the fading moon.

Safe in their beds

they lay down

their heads

and secretly whisper . . .

Night-night.

See you soon.